Head, Shoulders, Knees and Toes

WRITTEN BY **Skye Silver**

ILLUSTRATED BY **Mariana Ruiz Johnson**

SUNG BY **Chris Mears**

Barefoot Books
step inside a story

Head, shoulders, Knees and toes!
Head, shoulders, Knees and toes!
Eyes and ears and mouth and nose —
This is how your body grows.

Let's get a healthy start today.
Fresh and clean, that's the way!

Wash your hands and shake them dry.
Shake them low and shake them high.

Let's all shake them! Don't be shy.
Shake them low and shake them high!

Let's find something good to eat.

Yummy food, oh, what a treat!

Humming with a happy hum,
Rub your tummy and say "Yum!"

Crunching, munching every crumb,
Rub your tummy and say "Yum!"

On our way to school, we like to share.
Kindness shows our friends we care.

When your school friends all arrive,
Give each one a big high-five.

Sharing kindness, smiling wide,
Give your friends a big high-five!

We all love to play outside!

Jump, shout, stretch and slide.

Reaching up and reaching down,
Turn your body all around.

Can you touch your fingers to the ground?
Turn your body all around!

It's storytime — just what we need!
Choose a picture book to read.

Gather round the story rug.
Give your listening ears a tug.

All together feeling snug,
Give your listening ears a tug!

Time to wind down from the day,

And take it easy after play.

Let's curl up and get some sleep.
Breathe in slow and breathe in deep.

Let your breath out, soft and sweet.

Breathe in slow and breathe in deep.

Head, shoulders, knees and toes!
Head, shoulders, knees and toes!

Eyes and ears and mouth and nose —
This is how your body grows.

Healthy Habits for Your Growing Body!

Hygiene

Did you know that germs, bacteria and viruses (things that make us sick) wind up on our bodies every day? Thankfully, by keeping your body, hair, teeth and nails clean, which we call having good hygiene, you can prevent illnesses. Washing your hands after you use the toilet and before eating is one of the most important things you can do to keep yourself and those around you healthy.

Your turn! To make sure you're washing your hands long enough, sing the alphabet from A to Z while you wash. Then rinse and dry carefully.

Healthy food

Food is fuel for our bodies! Some foods are better for your body than others because they give your body more vitamins, minerals and protein — nutrients you need in order to move, breathe, keep warm, heal when you get sick and build strong bones. Including healthy foods like vegetables, fruits and whole grains in your diet will give you energy and help you feel your best!

Your turn! Try filling half your plate with bright fruits and vegetables. Can you eat a rainbow of foods?

Exercise

Moving our bodies is good for our health for many reasons. When you stretch, run, play on the playground, participate in sports, dance or do any movement activity, you strengthen your bones and muscles and even lower your chances of getting certain diseases. Plus, exercise can help you sleep better and feel happier!

Your turn! Ask a grown-up to help you record how much time you spend doing physical activity one day. Any type of exercise or active play counts. Aim for 30 minutes or more!

Kindness towards others

Believe it or not, being kind to other people is good for our bodies! When you do kind things, your brain releases a chemical called serotonin that makes you feel happier and even makes your heart healthier. And, of course, kindness makes other people feel good too.

Your turn! Find something caring you can do every day! You could play with a child who seems lonely, comfort a friend who is sad or help your family with chores at home. There are so many ways to be kind to others.

Reading

Being healthy means taking care of our bodies and our minds. Reading is like exercise for your brain. When you read or listen to stories, your memory gets a workout, which helps it grow stronger. Reading regularly also helps you learn new words and teaches your brain how to think about complicated ideas. Now that's smart!

Your turn! Even if you don't know how to read on your own, you can look at the pictures in books and tell your own stories. Visit the children's section of your local library to find a whole world of books to read!

Sleep

Sleep gives our bodies a chance to rest and our brains a chance to sort out everything we've learned during the day. Getting enough sleep can help put you in a good mood and make you less likely to get sick.

Your turn! Make sure you get a good night's sleep! If you have trouble sleeping, you can try gentle stretching, deep breathing, reading or listening to a story to help your body rest.

Head, Shoulders, Knees and Toes

♩=120

Head, shoul-ders, knees and toes (knees and toes!) Head, shoul-ders, knees and toes (knees and toes!)

Eyes and - ears and - mouth - and - nose, This is how your bo-dy grows (bo-dy grows!)

For Elias
— S. S.

To Pato, Pepo
and Felix, my family
— M. R. J.

Barefoot Books
2067 Massachusetts Ave
Cambridge, MA 02140

Barefoot Books
29/30 Fitzroy Square
London, W1T 6LQ

Text copyright © 2020 by Skye Silver. Illustrations copyright © 2020 by Mariana Ruiz Johnson
The moral rights of Skye Silver and Mariana Ruiz Johnson have been asserted

Lead vocals by Chris Mears. Musical arrangement © 2020 by Mike Flannery
Produced, mixed and mastered by Jumping Giant, New York City, USA
Animation by Collaborate Agency, UK

First published in United States of America by Barefoot Books, Inc
and in Great Britain by Barefoot Books, Ltd in 2020. All rights reserved

Graphic design by Sarah Soldano, Barefoot Books
Edited and art directed by Kate DePalma, Barefoot Books
Educational notes by Stefanie Paige Wieder, M.S.Ed., Child Development Expert
Reproduction by Bright Arts, Hong Kong
Printed in China on 100% acid-free paper
This book was typeset in Kidprint MT and PhoenixChunky
The illustrations were prepared in mixed media combined
with digital techniques

Hardback with enhanced CD ISBN 978-1-64686-068-5
Paperback with enhanced CD ISBN 978-1-64686-069-2
E-book ISBN 978-1-64686-085-2

British Cataloguing-in-Publication Data: a catalogue record for this book
is available from the British Library

Library of Congress Cataloging-in-Publication Data
is available upon request

1 3 5 7 9 8 6 4 2

Go to **www.barefootbooks.com/headshoulders** to access
your audio singalong and video animation online.

Barefoot Books
step inside a story

At Barefoot Books, we celebrate art and story that opens the hearts and minds of children from all walks of life, focusing on themes that encourage independence of spirit, enthusiasm for learning and respect for the world's diversity. The welfare of our children is dependent on the welfare of the planet, so we source paper from sustainably managed forests and constantly strive to reduce our environmental impact. Playful, beautiful and created to last a lifetime, our products combine the best of the present with the best of the past to educate our children as the caretakers of tomorrow.

www.barefootbooks.com

Skye Silver is an author and editor of books for young people. She has also written *Dump Truck Disco* and *Baby Play* for Barefoot Books. Skye lives in Boston, Massachusetts, USA, with her family, where the best part of her busy day is reading with her young son.

Mariana Ruiz Johnson is an award-winning children's book illustrator and author. She has also illustrated *The Last Hazelnut* for Barefoot Books. Mariana lives on the outskirts of Buenos Aires, Argentina, with her husband and two children.

As a child growing up in England, **Chris Mears** bought his first musical instrument at eleven: a bright red beat-up old surf-rock guitar. Learning to play it set him on a path through composing, recording and performing music that he is still continuing to explore. Today Chris is a media composer living in Lexington, Kentucky, USA, with his wife and two children.